I0757482

Boo Who

Written By

Michelle Beetz

Illustrated By

Minahal Aziz

Deep in a forest where fireflies flew,
Lived a small, gentle ghost with a soft little "boo!

While big ghosts howled and zoomed in the sky,
Boo flopped and fluttered—and barely got by.

He tripped on his sheet and spun like a top,
Then tumbled down soft in a pumpkin patch plop!

He squeaked when he spoke, and he glowed when he frowned.
The other ghosts laughed, floating circles around.

"You're not very spooky," they'd giggle and grin.
"More cuddly than creepy, and scared of the wind!"

Boo tried to be spooky. He tried to be loud.
But his hiccups made glitter. He stood out in a crowd.

So on Halloween night, Boo stayed out of sight.
"I'll just float in the trees. I'm not spooky... that's right."

He watched from a branch as the ghost parade flew.
Their whooshing and wailing made quite a loud boo!

Then Boo heard a sound—was that a small sniff?
He peeked through the leaves and gave his sheet a lift.

A kid in a cape sat alone on a log,
With one broken wand and a costume-drenched dog.

"My friends ran ahead," said the kid with a sigh.
"My candy spilled out, and I still want to cry."

Boo didn't know how to fix the sad scene,
But he fluffed up his sheet and tried to look clean.

He offered a smile and gave her a glow—
Not spooky or loud, just soft and hello.

The girl giggled once. "You're the nicest I've met."
"You're like a Halloween flashlight—but better than that!"

"Come on," Boo said. "We can find your crew!"
"I'm not very scary—but I'm great at boo!"

They passed sleepy pumpkins and bats in a swirl,
The dog found a donut, and gave it a twirl.

They tiptoed past skeletons juggling hats,
And waved at a trio of roller-skate bats.

The girl held Boo's hand. Boo glowed like the moon.
"I'm glad that I found you," she hummed a sweet tune.

Then suddenly—voices! The air filled with cheers!
Her friends had returned with wide grins and big ears.

"There you are!" they all shouted. "We looked everywhere!"
"Your wand's kinda broken. You've got glitter in your hair!"

Then they saw Boo and blinked once or twice.
"He's not very spooky... but wow, he's so nice!"

"You helped our friend find her way through the night.
That's the best kind of Boo—gentle and bright."

Boo wiggled and blushed. He'd never felt proud.
Before this whole night, he just blended with clouds!

Now every Halloween, ghosts float and say—
"Let's follow Boo Who... he'll light up the way!"

He didn't need growls or thunderous roars.
Just kindness and courage—those opened more doors.

He didn't need fangs or a big, spooky shout.
His gentle glow showed what Halloween's about.

The friends trick-or-treated from door after door,
And Boo lit the path like never before.

He didn't feel different, or awkward, or small
He felt like himself. And that beat them all.

From then on, Boo glowed wherever he went
Not from fear or from fumbles, but from being content.

And each Halloween, kids whisper it true:
"There's nothing quite kinder than a gentle 'Boo!'"

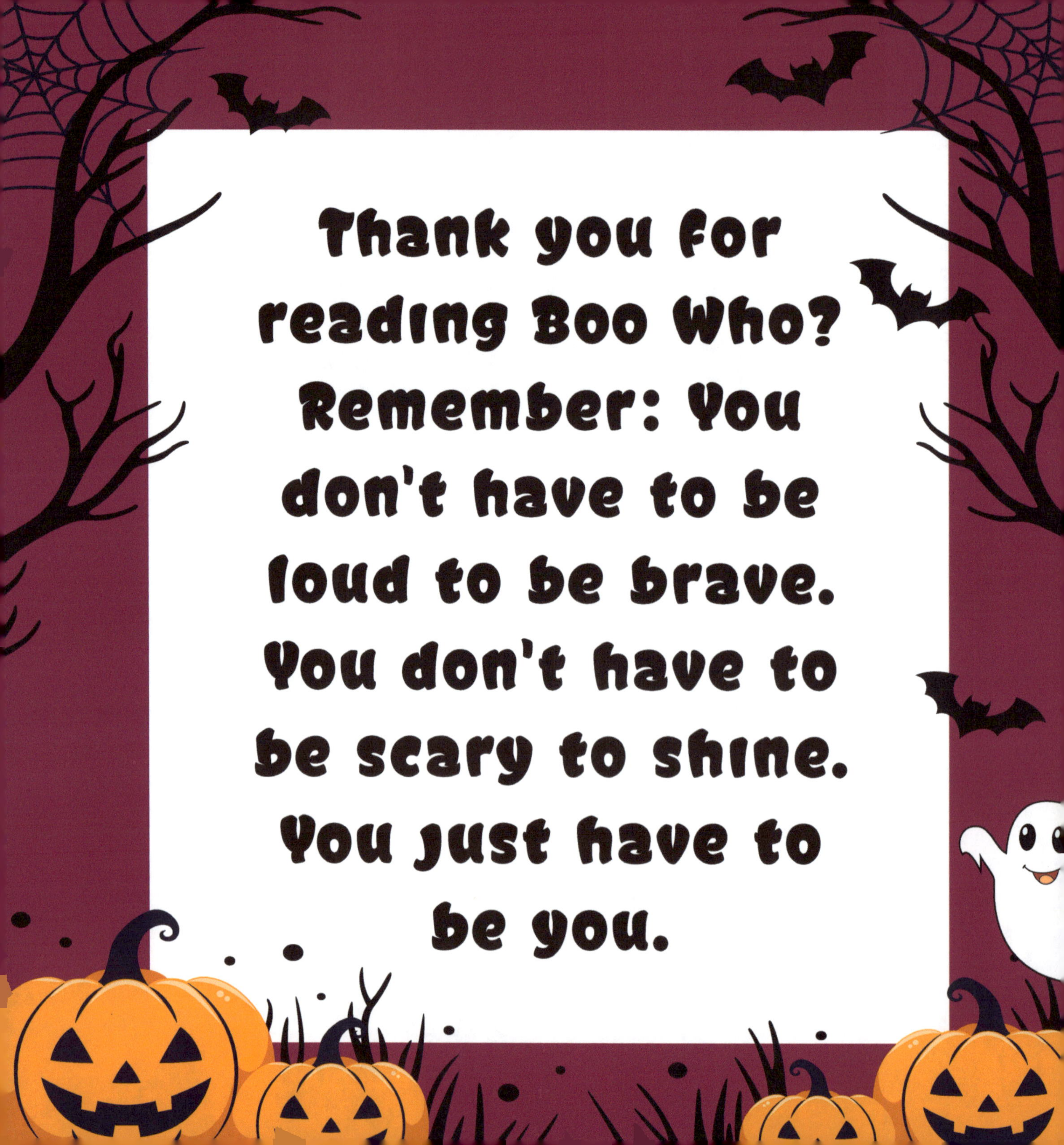

Thank you for reading Boo Who? Remember: You don't have to be loud to be brave. You don't have to be scary to shine. You just have to be you.

OFFICIAL
KIND GHOST
CLUB MEMBER
THIS CERTIFICATE IS PRESENTED TO

Let Your Kindness Shine!

Boo's Magic Words
Kind
Silly
Shy
Helpful
BOO-tiful
Brave
Sweet
Friend
Happy

Draw Your Own
Friendly Ghost!

(Make it silly, sweet, or spooky—just like Boo!)

Thank you for reading

Boo Who?

I hope you learned
that being kind is the
best kind of magic.

This Book Belongs To

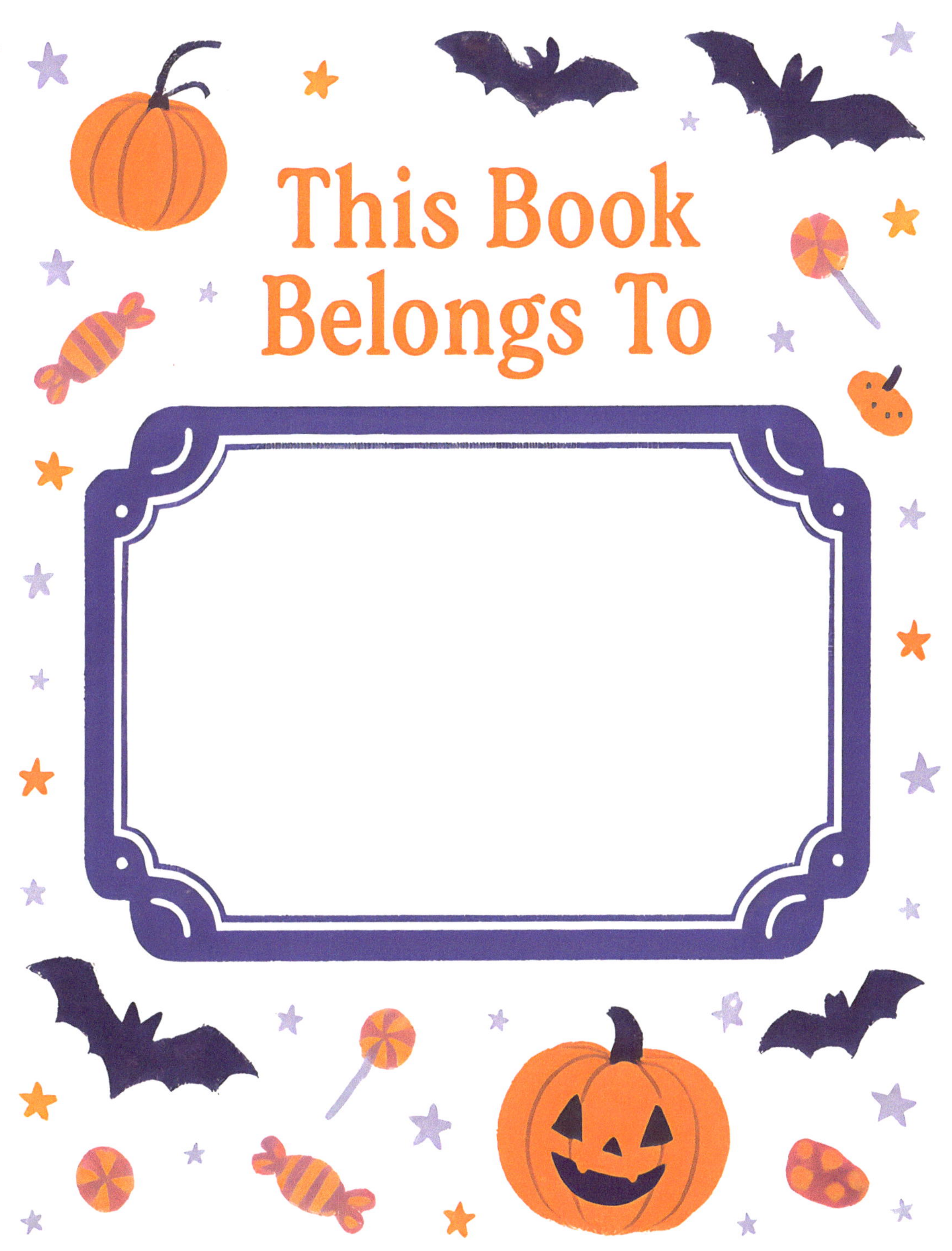

ISBN (Hardcover): 979-8-9996199-7-6

Printed in the United States of America.